INDIANA JONES™

AND THE SARGASSO PIRATES

PART 2

STORY
KARL KESEL

PENCIL BREAKDOWNS
KARL KESEL

INKS & FINISHES
EDUARDO BARRETO

COLORS
BERNIE MIREAULT

LETTERS
PAT BROSSEAU

COVER ART
ALEX ROSS

VISIT US AT
www.abdopublishing.com

Reinforced library bound edition published in 2011 by Spotlight, a division of the ABDO Group, 8000 West 78th Street, Edina, Minnesota 55439. Spotlight produces high-quality reinforced library bound editions for schools and libraries. Published by agreement with Dark Horse Comics, Inc., and Lucasfilm Ltd.

Printed in the United States of America, Melrose Park, Illinois.
052010
092010
 This book contains at least 10% recycled materials.

Library of Congress Cataloging-in-Publication Data

Kesel, Karl.
Indiana Jones and the Sargasso pirates / script [by] Karl Kesel ; art [by] Eduardo Barreto.
p. cm. -- (Indiana Jones and the Sargasso pirates ; 4)
Summary: When Indiana Jones signs on with a band of pirates, he does not realize that his old nemesis is among them.
ISBN 978-1-59961-761-9 (volume 1) -- ISBN 978-1-59961-762-6 (volume 2) -- ISBN 978-1-59961-763-3 (volume 3) -- ISBN 978-1-59961-764-0 (volume 4)
1. Graphic novels. [1. Graphic novels. 2. Adventure and adventurers--Fiction. 3. Pirates--Fiction. 4. Sea stories.] I. Barreto, Eduardo, ill. II. Title.
PZ7.7.K47 2011
741.5'973--dc22

2010006485

All Spotlight books have reinforced library bindings and are manufactured in the United States of America.

SHIP AFTER SHIP-- EMPTY!
EVERY USEFUL ARTICLE MISSING!
EVERY MORSEL OF FOOD GONE!
HOPE TURNS TO FATIGUE... HUNGER... DESPAIR...

NOT A SMOKED SAUSAGE! NOT A SOUP BONE! NOT EVEN A MOLDY PIECE OF CHEESE I'M NOT PARTICULARLY FOND OF!
OH, CRUEL FATE! I SHALL SURELY STARVE!

THESE BOATS, INDY... I DUNNO...
...COULD PEOPLE BE LIVING HERE?
MORE LIKELY NEARBY ISLANDERS RAID THIS PLACE, SELLING WHAT THEY CAN AS SCRAP AND SOUVENIRS.
AND THAT MEANS THERE'S A WAY OU--

HEY!
THAT'S A SPANISH GALLEON AND AN ENGLISH MAN-O'-WAR!
BUT THOSE SHIPS WOULD HAVE TO BE OVER THREE HUNDRED YEARS OLD!

BITTER EN'MIES FROM THE LOOKS, eh, DIGGER?
WONDERS WHO WAS LAST MAN STANDIN' THAT TIME...
ENGLAND. IT WAS HER FIRST TIME AT SEA, MORE OR LESS.
HOW COULD THESE SHIPS STILL BE HERE, LAWTON?

THE SARGASSO'S WEEDS TRAPS 'EM ...AN' THE SAME THICK WEEDS KEEPS 'EM FROM SINKIN.'
BEEN THAT WAY SINCE MAN FIRST MADE A BOX WHAT FLOATS.

THEN THERE COULD BE ALL KINDS OF SHIPS HERE!
ROMAN GALLEYS... uh... PHOENICIAN BIREMES... TRIREMES... EGYPTIAN--
WHAT IS THIS, JONES-- STUDY HOUR?

I CAN NAME THE KIND OF BOAT I'M INTERESTED IN REAL EASY--ONE THAT'LL GET US OUT OF THIS PLACE!

THIS IS AN IMPORTANT ARCHAEOLOGICAL FIND, CAIRO!
SURE, INDY-- AND WE HAVE TO FIND SOME FOOD AND FIND A WAY OUT, OR SOMEONE IS GONNA FIND US DEAD!

THOSE WRECKS PROB'LY BEEN PLUNDERED LONG AGO A' THE TRINKETS YOU WANTS, DIGGER.
UNLESS YER PLANNIN' TA STOW A WHOLE GALLEON IN YER PACK!

I REALLY HATE TO SAY THIS, BUT...
...YOU'RE RIGHT, LAWTON.
YOU TOO, CAIRO.
WE'VE GOT ENOUGH TO WORRY ABOUT RIGHT NOW.

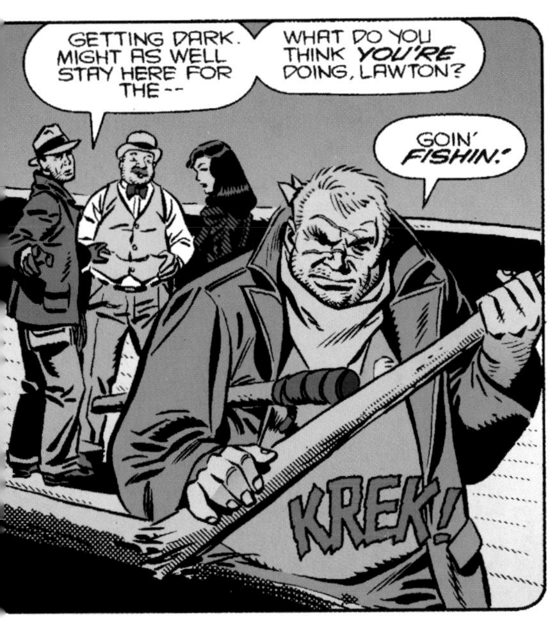
GETTING DARK. MIGHT AS WELL STAY HERE FOR THE--
WHAT DO YOU THINK YOU'RE DOING, LAWTON?
GOIN' FISHIN'!
KREK!

THE HULL A' THIS BEAUTY'S ROTTED THROUGH. SHOULD BE TEEMIN' WITH CATCH.
LET THE GIRLIE AN' GRIFTER PULLS UP PLANKIN' FER FIREWOOD. YOU COMES WITH ME, DIGGER.

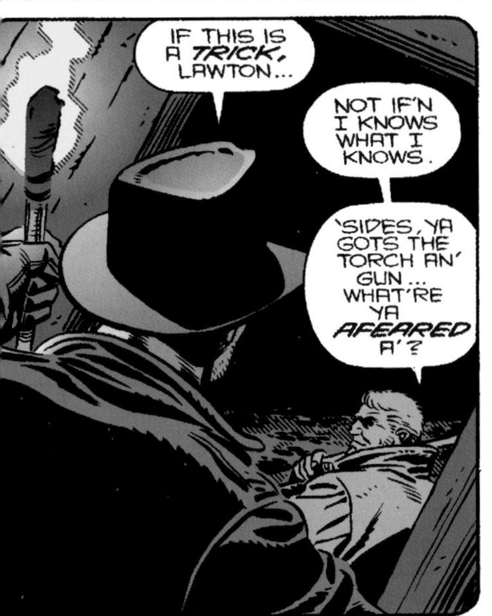
IF THIS IS A TRICK, LAWTON...
NOT IF'N I KNOWS WHAT I KNOWS.
'SIDES, YA GOTS THE TORCH AN' GUN... WHAT'RE YA AFEARED A'?

SNAKES!
THIS PLACE IS FULL OF SNAKES!

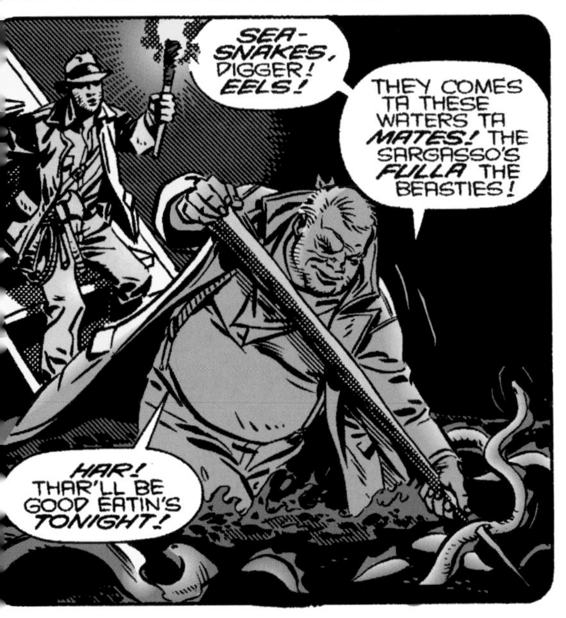
SEA-SNAKES, DIGGER! EELS!
THEY COMES TA THESE WATERS TA MATES! THE SARGASSO'S FULLA THE BEASTIES!
HAR! THAR'LL BE GOOD EATIN'S TONIGHT!

...DELECTABLE! NOT UNLIKE CHICKEN!
I DON'T KNOW HOW YOU COULD HAVE PASSED THIS UP, INDY.
WELL, THIS, uh, SEAWEED'S REALLY FILLING STUFF.

REST ASSURED YOUR PORTION DIDN'T GO TO WASTE!
Urrp!
SPEAKING OF REST...
COME, CAIRO-- OUR CABIN AWAITS! IT HAS AN OCEAN VIEW...

TAKE A HIKE, NEW JERSEY!
THE DEAL WAS, YOU'D GET ME TO NEW YORK CITY... THIS ISN'T EVEN ONE OF ITS BOROUGHS!
ALL BETS ARE OFF. FIND SOME ONE ELSE TO PLAY YOUR PAPER DOLL.

CAIRO, YOU'RE SUCH AN AMUSING LITTLE CREA- TURE...
YOU HEARD HER, NEW JERSEY.
THIS IS HOW IT'S GONNA BE--SHE GETS THE CABIN, THE THREE OF US SLEEP OUT HERE.

I'S USIN' THIS FRESH WATER TA CLEANS OUT ME SHOULDER, DIGGER.
THE GIRLIE PLUGGED ME BACKS ON THE NORMANDIE. BULLET SHOT CLEAN THROUGH, BUT...
WELL, YA DOESN'T WANT TA MAKES ME LOSE ME ARM, TOO, DOES YA?

THANK GOD I DON'T HAVE TO SLEEP IN THIS OUTFIT AGAIN!
GOTTA KEEP YOUR TOOLS SHARP, GIRL--NEVER KNOW WHEN THEY MIGHT BE USEFUL.
NOW, IF ONLY THIS HEAP WERE HAUNTED BY AN OLD LAUNDRYMAN WHO--

FUNNY-- THOUGHT I HEARD SOME- THING OUT HERE.
PROBABLY JUST INDY AND THE OTHERS. HARD TO TELL WHAT'S COMING FROM WHERE IN THIS FOG...

ZZZZZ
KREEENK

YI! YI! YI! YI! YI!

BLAM!
BLAM!

WH-
HUHN?
TOK!

THROWS ME A *WEAPON*, DIGGER!
WE'S ALL DEAD BY DAWN IF'N YA *DON'TS!*

NOW, NOW, MY GOOD MAN -- I'M SURE WE CAN WORK THINGS OUT!
MY LIFE IN EXCHANGE FOR, SAY, THIS EXQUISITE FACSIMILE OF A FINE POCKET WATCH?

DON'T JUST *STAND* THERE, YOU SPINELESS SAP!
GRAB HIS *SWORD!*
WHAM!

THIS DOESN'T LOOK *GOOD*, LAWTON! ANY *SUGGES-TIONS?*
FIGHTS 'TIL THAR'S NOT A DROP A' *BLOOD* IN YER VEINS!
ANY *OTHER* SUGGESTIONS?

I RECOMMEND *SURRENDER*, GENTS, OR THE PRETTY ONE'S SMILE WILL BE EAR TO EAR.
INDY, I'M *SORRY...*

OKAY -- EVERYONE TAKE IT EASY.
WE'LL JUST PUT OUR WEAPONS DOWN, AND...

LAWTON!

WHHHHHH
SNAK!

TUNGK!

IT'S OKAY! WE GIVE UP!
DON'T WE, LAWTON?

LASH THEM TIGHT, MEIN SEERAUBERS. VE DON'T VANT ANY DRIFTING OFF BETWEEN HERE UND THE BAY.
SHOULD'R KILLED YA ON THE ICEBERG, DIGGER... SAVED US ALL A SEA A' TROUBLES!

STEP LIVELY! YE BE GUESTS OF THE SARGASSO PIRATES NOW!
QUARTER-MASTER SEGAR SETS THE PACE...

PUT MY MIND AT EASE, LAWTON.
WHEN YOU THREW THAT AX, YOU WERE AIMING AT THE PIRATE, RIGHT? NOT AT YOURS TRULY.
ONE WAY'R T'OTHER, GIRLIE...
...IT WOULD'
SOLVED TH
PROBLEM.

PIRATES CAPTURE INDY, COMPANIONS!

PRISONERS TAKEN DEEP INTO MIST-SHROUDED SARGASSO!

ESCAPE--IMPOSSIBLE!

DESTINATION--?

WELCOME VISITORS, TO SARGASSO BAY-- THE CITY OF SHIPS!

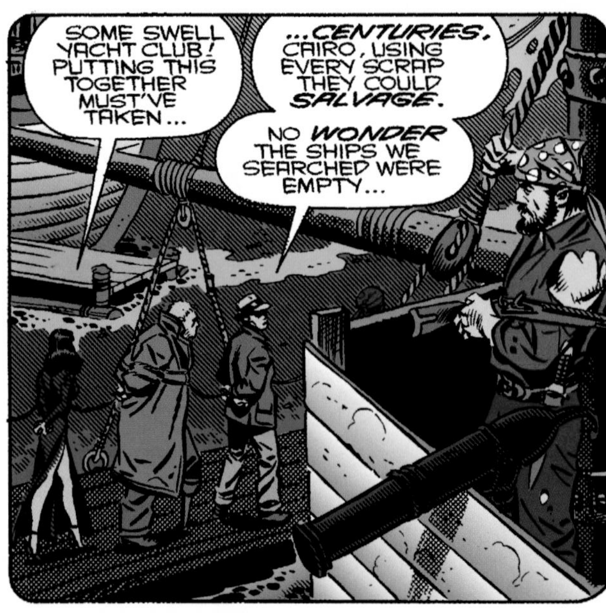

SOME SWELL YACHT CLUB! PUTTING THIS TOGETHER MUST'VE TAKEN...
...CENTURIES, CAIRO, USING EVERY SCRAP THEY COULD SALVAGE.
NO WONDER THE SHIPS WE SEARCHED WERE EMPTY...

EVEN THESE MEAGER ATTEMPTS AT CIVILIZATION GLADDEN MY HEART!
SHORT OF ESCAPIN
THIS OCEAN, I'M SUR
I COULD LEAD A LON
PROSPEROUS LIFE HERE...
THAT, FETTMOPS, VILL BE DECIDED BY THE SEA WITCH!

YOU MUST BE JOKING. "THE SEA WITCH"?
LEADER OF THE SARGASSO PIRATES, FRAULEIN.
ABLE TO CALL UP THE BEASTS OF THE DEEP!

YE'LL MEET HER, VISITORS. AYE -- SOONER THAN WISHED.
TODAY WE MUST TRY TO EARN PASSAGE ON THE DECKS OF HER EBONY SHIP, THE FREEDOM.

SINGLE LINE! BACKS STRAIGHT! THESE PROCEEDINGS NOW BE OPEN!

OBVIOUSLY, NONE OF THESE VISITORS WILL LIVE TO EARN PASSAGE. BETTER THEY BE CHAINED IN HOT STEEL-- BUT SHIP'S ARTICLES FORBID THE SEA WITCH EVEN THAT MERCY!
THIS ONE WILL DISPENSE HER DUTIES. MAKE READY TO DISPENSE THE BODIES..

FROM WHERE D'YE HAIL?
ANSWER SMART! THE SEA WITCH COMMANDS IT!
Ah... JONES IS THE NAME-- NEW JERSEY JONES! I'M ONE OF THE JONES BOYS!

I MUST SAY YOU HAVE A LOVELY COMMUNITY HERE, MISS WITCH, AND--
WHAT MY... FRIEND MEANS IS WE DON'T WANT TO CAUSE ANY TROUBLE.
WE COME FROM... FAR LANDS, AND--

NOTS ME, DIGGER.
BILL LAWTON HAILS FROM THE SEA.

UNLASH THE ONE-LEGGER.
HIS WORDS MARK HIM ONE OF US.

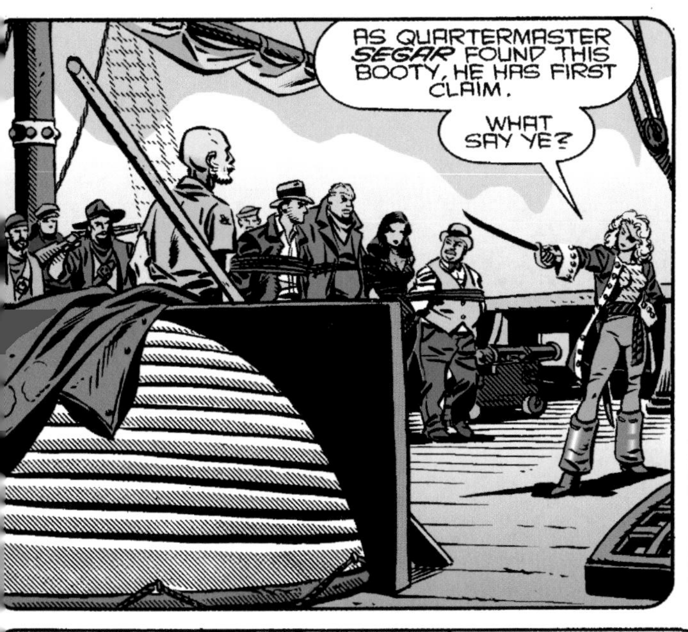
AS QUARTERMASTER SEGAR FOUND THIS BOOTY, HE HAS FIRST CLAIM.
WHAT SAY YE?

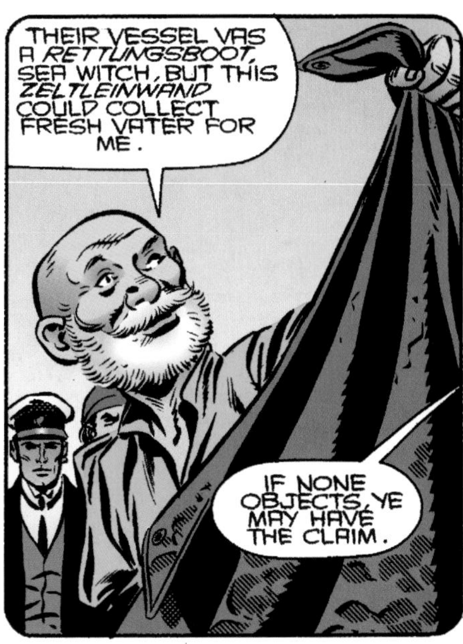
THEIR VESSEL VAS A RETTUNGSBOOT, SEA WITCH, BUT THIS ZELTLEINWAND COULD COLLECT FRESH VATER FOR ME.
IF NONE OBJECTS, YE MAY HAVE THE CLAIM.

THE ONE CALLED LAWTON--YE HAVE EARNED PASSAGE BY FEALTY TO THE SEA. YE ARE WELCOMED TO OUR RANKS.
THE SEA WITCH GRANTS YE A CLAIM, ALSO.

I WANTS THE GUN...
...AN' THE GIRLIE!

THE PISTOL YE MAY HAVE, BUT NOT THE WOMAN.
THE SARGASSO SHACKLES OUR LIBERTY ENOUGH. WE WILL NOT ADD THE CHAINS OF SLAVERY.
THE SEA WITCH WILL GRANT YE A CLAIM OF THE FAIR ONE'S PASSAGE, INSTEAD.

UNLASH HER, BOS'N.

WAIT! WE'RE TRAVELING TOGETHER! TELL THE GOOD LADY, CAIRO!
DID I MENTION I'M FROM THE SEA, TOO?
YO-HO-HO! BRING THE PORT TO STARBOARD! SCUTTLE THE BILGE!
THE TIME FOR SUCH ANTICS HAS PASSED... IF IT EXISTED AT ALL.
YE BOTH REMAINING MUST NOW CHOOSE A TEST-- WET OR DRY.
SUCCEED AND YE JOIN US... BUT FAILURE IS DEATH, SLOW AND HORRIBLE...

WHAT BE EACH OF YE'S DECISION-- WET OR DRY?
THE SEA WITCH GROWS IMPATIENT!

GEE--SHE MADE THEM BOTH SOUND SO APPEAL-ING.
CHANCES ARE THE WET TEST HAS SOMETHING TO DO WITH THESE EEL-INFESTED WATERS.
ME, I'M FOR THE DRY...

SO IT BE DECIDED!
THE WET TEST FOR THE FAT ONE...
...AND THE DRY TEST FOR YE!

BUT... WE DIDN'T... THAT WASN'T... YOU DON'T...
PREPARE THE RUMFUSTIAN!
AND BRING THE STUTTERING ONE TO THE KRAKEN'S PIT!

THE KRAKEN'S PIT! A DEADLY TEST INDY MUST PASS...OR DIE TRYING!
WALK THE PLANK?
Um...YOU DO KNOW, DON'T YOU? --HISTORICALLY, PIRATES DIDN'T DO THIS...

CERTAINLY. BUT SO MANY VISITORS SEEMED TO EXPECT IT, THIS ONE DIDN'T WANT TO DISAPPOINT THEM.
OF COURSE, YE DON'T WALK THE PLANK PROPER...

...YE LEAPS FROM HERE TO ONE OF YON BOARDS.
THE CHASM IS GREAT ENOUGH, AYE, BUT THE TRICK IS REACHING A PLANK NOT ROTTED THROUGH.

I GET IT. THE "DRY" TEST. I HAVE TO KEEP DRY. WHAT IF I END UP IN THE WATER?
THEN IT'S THE KRAKEN FOR YE...

WUU-OOOM!
WUU-OOOM!
SHE CALLS THE BEAST...

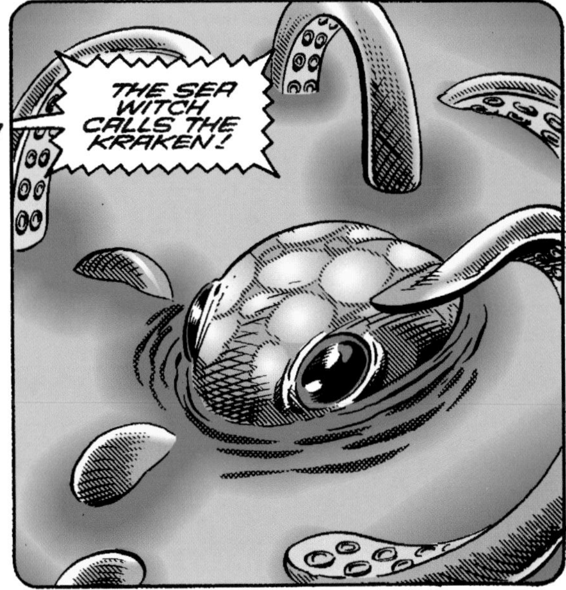
THE SEA WITCH CALLS THE KRAKEN!

LOOKIT THEM *TENTACLES* THRASHIN' THE WATERS...
KIND'R LIKE *SNAKES*, eh, DIGGER?
I... uh... I'VE SEEN BIGGER...

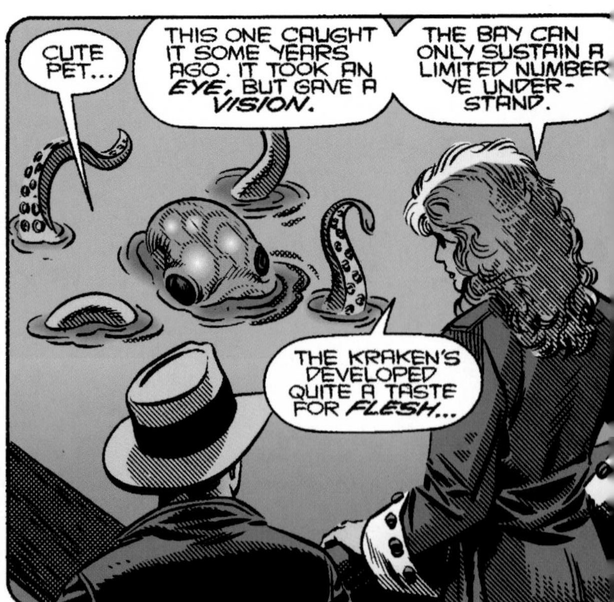
CUTE PET...
THIS ONE CAUGHT IT SOME YEARS AGO. IT TOOK AN *EYE*, BUT GAVE A *VISION*.
THE BAY CAN ONLY SUSTAIN A LIMITED NUMBER YE UNDER-STAND.
THE KRAKEN'S DEVELOPED QUITE A TASTE FOR *FLESH*...

WHAT IF I REFUSE TO JUMP?
THE SEA WITCH SHOOTS YE IN BOTH KNEES, AND YE ARE DROPPED INTO THE BEAST'S WAITING MAW.

JUST ASKING.
NEVER WAS MU GOOD A MULTIPL CHOICE

KOOONK!

HEY! CAN I *PICK* 'EM, OR--

K-KRAKK!

SPLUSH!

GHAH!

Ngh!

SPAK! SPAK!
SPAK!

PAK!
POOSH! POOSH!

BLOOD ON THE WATER...
HAR! IF'N THAR'S A TAVERN IN PORT, ME BULLY BOYS, FIRST ROUND'S ON BILL LAWTON!

WAIT.

AGK!
KAK! KAK!

IT'S... NOT DEAD... BUT...
...I DON'T THINK YOUR... PET'S... COMIN' BACK... SOON...

ONLY ONE OTHER HAS BESTED THE KRAKEN BEFORE, VISITOR. YE HAVE EARNED PASSAGE, INDEED.
BOS'N-- HELP HIM FROM THE PIT.

INDY! ARE YOU OKAY?
JUST A... FEW INCHES TALLER, CAIRO, THAT'S ALL...
WHAT ABOUT NEW JERSEY?
WHAT KIND OF TWISTED TORTURES ARE THEY PUTTING HIM THROUGH?

INDY--THE WET TEST IS A DRINKING CONTEST!
RUMFUSTIAN IS A TORTURE OF ABOUT 120 PROOF!

...YA DON' UNNER-STAN', CAP'N. BEASHES... BEASHES'RE LIKE... DECKS... LOSSA DECKS... AN' MOUNT'INS...
...MOUNT'INS, AS I'S TELLIN' THE 'LEDGED RUMFOOSHIN CHAMP'N HERE, MOUNT'INS...

...I'LL BRING ONE HERE, YESSA WILL... RIGH' HERE... GIMME A BOAT...
BRING THAT ONE TO MY QUARTERS TOMORROW, SEGAR...
...ONCE HE CAN STAND AGAIN.

GUTEN TAG, INDIANA! HOW ARE YOU DOING?
ES GEHT MIR GUT, SEGAR. BUT I WOULDN'T TURN DOWN A LITTLE SUN-SHINE.

GOT MY WHIP BACK AS MY CLAIM -- GUESS I'M NOT A VISITOR ANY-MORE, HUH?
HERE THERE ARE ONLY VISITORS UND SEABORN.
I MYSELF HAFF BEEN VISITING SINCE 1916.

<U-BOAT CAPTAIN? I RECOGNIZE THE INSIGNIA.> *
<YES. A DREAD-NOUGHT WOUNDED MY BOAT. WE ESCAPED, BUT BECAME HELPLESS AND DRIFTED HERE BEFORE HELP COULD ARRIVE.>
* TRANSLATED FROM GERMAN.

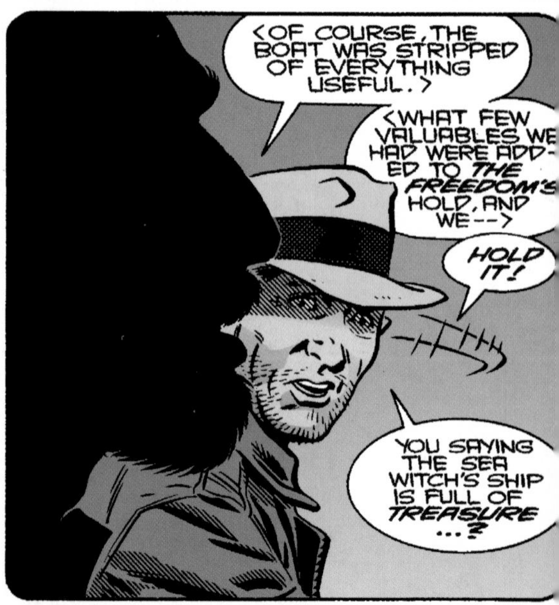
<OF COURSE, THE BOAT WAS STRIPPED OF EVERYTHING USEFUL.>
<WHAT FEW VALUABLES WE HAD WERE ADD-ED TO THE FREEDOM'S HOLD, AND WE-->
HOLD IT!
YOU SAYING THE SEA WITCH'S SHIP IS FULL OF TREASURE...?

JA, THE FREEDOM IS FILLED WITH BOOTY FROM EVERY SHIP IN THE SARGASSO. IT IS COMMON KNOWLEDGE.
THE VIKING AX I HAD--IS THAT THERE?

UND PIECES FROM ANCIENT GREECE, ROME, EGYPT...
THEY VILL MAKE US ALL RICH MEN IF... VHEN VE ESCAPE HERE.
EVERYONE VILL RECEIVE EQUAL SHARES--INCLUDING YOU, INDIANA.

I'VE GOTTA SEE THIS STUFF, SEGAR. ANY WAY YOU CAN GET ME IN?
NEIN! YOU VOULD HAFF TO TALK TO THE SEA WITCH HERSELF...

PERMISSION TO COME ON BOARD, SEA WITCH?
PERMISSION DENIED.

THOUGHT MAYBE I COULD PAY YOU BACK A LITTLE FOR SAVING MY LIFE AT THE KRAKEN'S PIT.
SEE, I BEEN AROUND THE WORLD--SEEN THINGS AND LANDS YOU CAN'T EVEN IMAGINE...

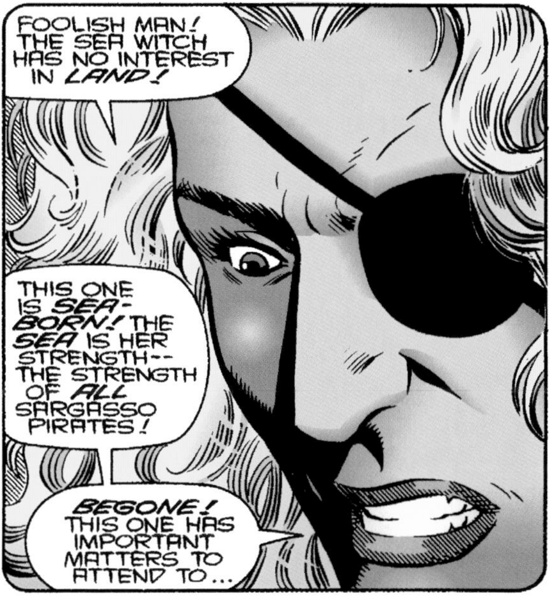
FOOLISH MAN! THE SEA WITCH HAS NO INTEREST IN LAND!
THIS ONE IS SEA-BORN! THE SEA IS HER STRENGTH-- THE STRENGTH OF ALL SARGASSO PIRATES!
BEGONE! THIS ONE HAS IMPORTANT MATTERS TO ATTEND TO...

SEA WITCH, MY DEAR -- I CAME AS SOON AS I GOT YOUR MESSAGE!
MANY THANKS, NEW JERSEY.
COME -- THIS ONE'S PRIVATE CHAMBERS ARE *AFT*...

THIS ONE DESIRES TO KNOW *ALL* ABOUT THAT WHICH SHE HAS NEVER SEEN -- LAND! MOUNTAINS! BEACHES!
BUT BE WARNED -- MY MEN MUST *NEVER* HEAR OF THIS!
OH, I WILL BE THE *ACME* OF DISCRETION, WITCHIE...

CAIRO! JUST THE PERSON I'M LOOKING FOR.
DO YOU KNOW WHAT'S IN THE SEA WITCH'S *SHIP?*

SURE. TREASURE GALORE. WE'RE ALL RICH AS ROCKEFELLER.
NOW I CAN BUY SOME OF THOSE *ROTTING OUTFITS* THAT'RE ALL THE RAGE IN THIS PLACE.

IF ONLY I COULD GET *IN*, THERE'RE PROBABLY ARTIFACTS DATING BACK *CENTURIES*...
JONES -- THIS OBSESSION OF YOURS IS *CHARMING*, BUT FIRST THINGS FIRST!
WE'RE *TRAPPED* HERE!

AND *THE FREEDOM*'S THE ONLY SHIP IN ANY CONDITION TO GET *OUT*.
LISTEN...

EVENIN', BOYS.

SO WHAT'S TO DO FOR FUN IN THIS BURG? CATCH A FLICK AT THE BIJOU? CUT A RUG WITH BENNY GOODMAN?
C'MON, FELLAS-- I DON'T BITE... MUCH.

DANCIN' SURE SOUNDS GOOD TO ME. USED TO DO IT FOR A LIVIN'... A LIFETIME AGO AND A HALF A WORLD AWAY.
ANY OF YOU SAILORS KNOW "THE ST. LOUIS BLUES"?

GULLY KNOWS A FEW SHAN-TIES...
CLOSE ENOUGH... BUT NOT HERE.
YOU BOYS HAVEN'T SEEN ME IN ACTION. WE NEED A MORE PRIVATE SETTING...

NO GUARDS.
CAIRO'S HOLDING UP HER END OF THE DEAL.

WISH I'D PAID MORE ATTENTION TO DR. WILSON'S PAPER ON GALLEON CONSTRUC-TION.
I THINK THIS IS THE ORLOP DECK... AND THAT DOOR SHOULD LEAD TO...

...THE TREASURE ROOM!

I KNOW MAJOR MUSEUMS WITH SMALLER COLLECTIONS THAN THIS.
GREEK... VENETIAN... MINOAN... EVERY WESTERN CULTURE THAT EVER SAILED THE SEA IS RIGHT HERE.
JUST ABOUT EVERY PIECE IS FILLED, TOO-- GOLD... PIECES OF EIGHT... JEWEL--

BLAM! BLAM!
THAT'S... MY GUN!
LAWTON!

AYE, IT'S MUTINY, WITCH, SWEET 'N' SIMPLE.
BILL LAWTON'S IN CHARGE NOW, AN' THEM WHAT DON'T AGREES...
...PAYS A PRICE A' BLOOD!

YE BE A FOOL, LAWTON! THE SARGASSO PIRATES WILL HAVE HEARD THE PISTOL SHOTS... THEY WILL RALLY TO THE SEA WITCH!
THIS MUTINY WILL BE BROKEN-- AND ALL OF YE ALONG WITH IT!

NOT IF'N YER DEAD, WITCH.

BLAM!
BLAM!
BLAM!
BLAM!

YE'LL... PAY FOR THIS...
STILL ALIVE, WITCH? EASY TA FIX THAT!

REMEMBERS, ME BULLY BOYS, YA SAW 'ER PULLS THE KNIFE ON ME.
THIS BE SELF-DEFENSE, CLEAR AS--

WWHHHHH
KRAK!

FUNNY-- DOESN'T LOOK LIKE SELF-DEFENSE TO *ME*, LAWTON.

WAS *YOU* THE ONE WHAT GOTS THE GUARDS AWAY, DIGGER? 'SPECTS THEY'S HAPPIER'N IF *I* DONE THE DEED.
THANK DR. JONES FER ME, BULLY BOYS.

KRISCH!

KRUNK!

SMASH!

YAARRRR!

PERHAPS THIS IS A GOOD TIME TO *REMIND* YOU, LORD-- ALL THOSE SCAMS AND SWINDLES...
...I LIKE TO THINK THOSE PEOPLE ARE *WISER* FOR HAVING KNOWN ME, DON'T YOU AGREE?
AH! A SIGN FROM *ABOVE!*

KRUMP!

Y'KNOW, I COULD *REALLY USE* THAT GUN, NEW JERSEY.
THIS GUN? OH, WELL, I SUPPOSE...

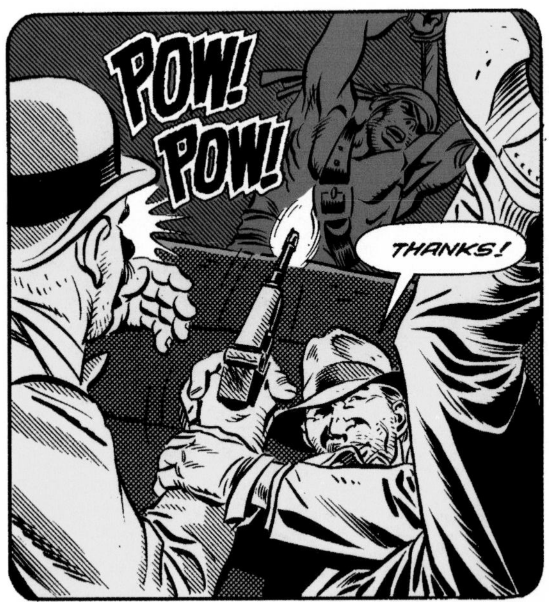
POW! POW!
THANKS!

YER A DEAD MAN, DIGGER! THAT LUGER ONLY HOLDS EIGHT ROUNDS...
...AN' BILL LAWTON GOTS YER OLD GUN AN' ALL THE BULLETS WHAT GOES WITH IT!
BLAM! BLAM!

THE SEA WITCH--?
I...uh... FEAR SHE'S DEAD, INDY!

WON'T DO ANY GOOD TO JOIN HER!
C'MON!
POW! POW! POW!

KK-TEESSHH!